A Turtle's

Magical

Adventure

Wanda Luthman

DEDICATION

To all the turtles who don't like their shells, may you find the grace to love yourself.

May you discover when you embrace your weakness, you make it your strength.

Also, I'd like to thank Sharon Lipman for the wonderfully inspired Cover Design and to my Editor, Eve Arroyo.

CONTENTS

FOREWORD

Our lives are stories. I've heard it said once that God loves stories and that's why He created humans. I love stories too. I love telling stories and I love hearing and reading stories. As a Counselor, I know that we tell ourselves our own stories throughout our lives but have you ever noticed how they change as we grow? Maybe not in big sweeping ways, but in small more subtle ways that make us feel different about our past and ourselves. Have you tried to re-write your story, changing something negative into the most positive, most powerful thing ever? Try it. I'm a Counselor by education, a Helper by calling and a Storyteller by inspiration. Have a story? Tell me. Want to read a story that will change you? Join me in *A Turtle's Magical Adventure*.

Wanda Luthman

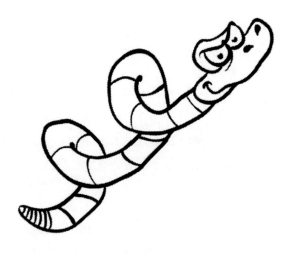

1 TAD

The morning sunshine danced off the ripples made in the pond of Timberwood Forest by Tad, the turtle. Tad was a tad too small, and a tad too shy to have any friends. So today, as most days, he played by himself. He didn't mind though, because he loved swimming. When he was on land, he felt slow and awkward, but when he was in the water, he felt amazing! In fact, nothing made him happier. He sang a song out loud that he had made up while he swam, "Swishing here, swishing there, I can swim anywhere."

A little corny perhaps, but it goes with my happy mood, he thought.

He dove deep down into the pond just to see if he could touch the bottom. He did it! Then, with one flip of his foot, he turned around and pushed off the pond floor toward the surface.

"*Ha, ha*," he laughed as his head came bursting out of the water. He played tag with a fish and swam in between the pond grass. By late morning, he was ready for a break. He crawled out of the water and onto the muddy bank of the pond. He spotted a warm rock to doze on and slowly made his way there. He used his small, webbed, front feet to pull himself up, and his slightly larger webbed back feet to push. Tad struggled this way for a few minutes because his webbed feet could not grab too well. Finally, he made it on top of the rock. There he dozed, warming in the sun. A few hours passed when his stomach began to growl. He decided to find something to eat.

As he was searching for some tender grass, he saw Mama Duck with her twelve quacking ducklings waddling single file behind her.

"Hello there, Tad," she greeted him.

"Good Morning, ma'am," he replied.

Tad found some sweet grass near an older turtle.

As they were eating, he asked her, "Why are turtles so slow on land?"

She thought for a minute and replied, "Tad, turtles aren't slow, it's just that the rest of the world is so fast."

Tad thought that didn't even make sense, but instead of saying so he mumbled, "I don't want to be slow, I want to be fast!"

"Tad, you'll find your rhythm to life," she replied comfortingly.

Tad finished his lunch in silence and went over by a tree to think about his troubles. A snake was going by and stopped when he saw Tad.

"What sseems to have sstolen your ssmile?" Steve the snake asked.

Tad replied, "I'm too slow."

Steve, who was always up to no good, was happy to find someone miserable. He said, "Well, Tad, you're problem iss obviouss."

Tad's interest was raised, "Do you know how to help me?"

"Yess, I ssuppose I do," said Steve, "it's your sshell that'ss sslowing you down. If you just didn't have your sshell, you would be as fasst as me." Steve slithered around quickly to show off his fastness, but the snake knew Tad couldn't live without his shell.

"Ssee, I don't have a sshell, and I'm very fast," Steve said.

"Oh, thank you, Steve, now I know how to fix my problem!" Tad said happily.

"You're welcome," said Steve as he

slithered away, smiling to himself knowing he created more misery for the little turtle.

Tad went to work right away. He tried pulling his arms and legs in and pushing himself out of his shell through his neck opening. That didn't work. He tried rolling over and rubbing the shell off his back. That didn't work. He tried knocking his shell against a rock.

One-two-three crash, one-two-three crash, one-two-three crash.

The commotion brought out a worm who lived under the rock.

"What is going on here?" Sherm the worm demanded.

"I'm trying to crack my shell," replied Tad.

"What in mercy's name for?" asked Sherm.

"I want to get rid of my shell so I can be as fast as a snake," explained Tad.

"Why do you want to be as fast as a snake?" asked Sherm.

"Because snakes go here and there so fast. They're free!" Tad said.

"Oh, I see," said Sherm. "While it is true snakes go here and there and seem to be free, they also have a thick skin to protect them from disease and predators. If you did not have your shell, you would be soft on the outside and could get sick or eaten by a bird. Your shell is your protection. In fact, I wish I had a shell. My only protection is when I'm crawling in the dirt or under a rock."

"I didn't realize the importance of my shell," Tad said, "but it doesn't bother you to be slow?"

"No, not really. I don't think about being slow. I have nowhere I need to be in a hurry. I enjoy being a worm and crawling along the dirt. I get to feel the cool wetness, and I like that. I smell my way along and sometimes I discover new and glorious smells. I like that too!" said Sherm.

Tad decided to go back in the pond where he

felt happiest and think about what Sherm had told him. Mama Duck and her twelve ducklings were swimming too.

"Mama Duck, do you ever wish you could walk faster?" asked Tad.

"Well, sometimes I think it would be nicer if I didn't have to waddle when I walk because that takes a lot of energy. But, I know that my feet are webbed and pointed inward so I can swim very well; it's a trade-off. I just enjoy the fun of what I can do and don't worry so much about what's difficult." Mama Duck replied.

"Thank you, Mama Duck," said Tad, and he swam off. He was happy to be swimming again, and happier still because he had a new appreciation for his webbed feet and his shell and what he could enjoy when he was on land. But, in the back of his mind lurked thoughts about what Steve had told him.

Tad went to sleep that night a little happier. He spent the rest of the summer swimming in the pond, enjoying the feel of the dirt on his belly when he crawled, and discovering new smells on land. The summer days turned into fall and it was time for him to begin school. He enjoyed learning and being with other animals from the forest, but he was always late because it took him a long time to crawl to school.

2 THE DEEP FOREST

His frustration with his slowness grew again. Mr. Peabody, the peacock, was Tad's teacher. He would scold Tad for being late and make him stay after school to make up for the time he missed. But, that would only make Tad even later getting home. The other forest animals in his class would make fun of him. Tad felt alone and different and he began hating his slowness.

One evening, crawling home from school after another day of punishment, Tad met

Steve the snake again.

"Hello there, my boy. I ssee you sstill have your sshell, iss that what'ss got you sso blue?" asked Steve.

"Yes, I hate being slow. I get in trouble every day at school because I'm late. All the forest animals at school make fun of me because I'm different. I can't take it anymore. I want to be rid of my shell once and for all!" Tad declared.

"I know how you can losse your sshell for good," replied Steve.

"Tell me, tell me, tell me!" Tad said excitedly.

Steve's voice grew soft, "There's a wizard deep in Timberwood Forest who can change you with his magic."

"How do I get there?" Tad asked

"The way will be hard. The way will be long. The way will be dangerouss," Steve cautioned.

"That's ok. It'll be worth it. Please tell me how to get there," Tad pleaded.

"Okay, then. You go to the third large oak and turn into the deep forest. At first, there will be many leaves. Passt those, you will ssee a dirt path. Follow that until you come to a river. Crosss the river and climb the hill on the other sside. You will ssee the tower in the treess. There iss where the wizard lives," explained Steve.

"Thank you, Steve. Thank you so much!" Tad said excitedly.

"Ssee you later, Tad," said Steve, who knew nothing good ever came from magic.

Ted crawled past the patches of beautiful fragrant lilacs to the third large oak as evening was approaching. The deep woods looked dark and scary and for a moment Tad almost turned back. But, in his head he heard forest animals laughing at him and Mr. Peabody scolding him and he felt even more determined to go see the wizard.

Past the third large oak and onto the leaves, Tad crawled. The leaves were crunching loudly beneath his feet and belly. He thought he'd never get through them. But, he kept putting one webbed foot in front of the other (like he heard in a song once) and finally he was onto the dirt path. The dirt path was cool and moist and he liked how it felt on his belly. He crawled on. The forest grew dark. There were sounds in the deep forest he wasn't used to, and to be honest they were scary. Just when he was feeling the most scared of all, a small light in the air flashed on and then off. Soon, there were other lights around him doing the same thing. There were small voices coming from these lights,

"Who's that?"

"What's that?"

"Who goes there?"

"What's going on?"

Tad said, "I'm Tad, the turtle, I'm going to

see the wizard."

"Oh my."

"Gee whiz."

"Uh oh."

"Ooooh," each light replied.

"Who are you?" asked Tad.

"We're lightning bugs."

"Oh yes, lightning bugs."

"Light up, bugs."

"Bugs that light up like lightning," the lights replied in turn.

"I've never seen anything like you before," Tad said marveling at them.

"We haven't seen anything like you before."

"Oh, no we haven't."

"You're strange."

"You're different," the lights said.

"I know I'm strange and different. That's why I'm going to see the wizard," said Tad.

"Strange isn't bad."

"No, different isn't bad."

"Unusual in a pleasant way."

"We like you," the lights said.

"Oh, I misunderstood then. My schoolmates don't like me because I'm strange and different," Tad explained.

"Oh, that's too bad."

"We're sorry."

"Schoolmates misunderstand."

"Maybe they're scared of different," the lights said comfortingly.

"Maybe so," Tad agreed. "Thanks for your understanding."

"No problem."

"Righty-O."

"You bet."

"You're welcome," the lights said.

Tad yawned and said, "I'm really tired but I'm really scared in the deep woods."

"Go to sleep."

"We'll watch you."

"We'll stay with you."

"We won't leave until morning," the lights promised.

3 THE MAGICAL TIMERWOOD FOREST

He began crawling along the path some more and soon he ran into a snail. As Tad approached, the snail pulled into her shell.

Tad said, "Hello."

But, the snail didn't reply. Instead she shuddered.

"Don't be afraid," Tad said. "I won't hurt you."

Tad waited. It was hard to be patient, but he knew from his own experience that was the only way someone will come out of their shell. He began to look around and up into the tall trees. He enjoyed the beauty of the sunshine filtered through the leaves. Finally, the snail peeked out from her shell.

"I'm Tad. I'm shy, too. What's your name?" asked Tad.

The snail said in a small and squeaky voice, "I'm Gail."

Tad continued, "Hi, Gail. Do you live here in the deep woods?"

"Yes, for now. Actually, I live wherever I go. I carry my home on my back," replied Gail.

"Oh, so you're at home wherever you go!" Tad said as if discovering something new.

"Well, yes, I suppose that's true," said Gail.

"I have a shell and carry my home with me, too! But, I sure don't feel at home in the deep woods," remarked Tad.

"I don't always feel at home wherever I'm at either," explained Gail, "but at least I have my home with me. I can go inside my shell and feel safe anytime I want."

"That's true," agreed Tad. "I never thought of that before."

Evermore on Tad's mind, he had to ask the question, "But, do you mind being slow?"

"*Hmmm*," Gail thought out loud for a moment, "Timing is everything. It's important to be on time. Sometimes, I have to plan months in advance to get to the pond for the summer. But, I don't mind planning ahead and I love the trip! The only time being slow is a disadvantage is when something fast is chasing me. And that's when I'm most thankful for my shell."

"That's a good point, Gail. But, if I didn't have my shell, I'd be able to run away from fast things chasing me. And running would feel so good," said Tad dreamily. "That's why I'm going to see the wizard. He's going to help me."

"I never thought of running. I'd be too

scared to live without my shell. I hope the wizard is helpful, but I've heard magic isn't good," cautioned Gail.

"What have you heard about magic," Tad asked.

"Oh, just that sometimes it goes terribly wrong," Gail replied.

"Thanks, Gail, I best be on my way. Bye," said Tad.

"Bye, Tad. Nice to meet you. Be careful," said Gail.

"I will," replied Tad.

Tad crawled along the dirt path thinking about how nice it was to have his home with him and what a good protection his shell provided him, but still wishing he could be faster.

The sun shone low on the horizon as he approached the river. The river was deep, fast and wide because there had been a lot of rain in the forest. Tad sighed. He enjoyed swimming but he had never swum in moving water. He was afraid, but didn't want to think about it right now. He needed to rest. He was tired and hungry. He had a long day of crawling along the ground. He looked around for some grass to munch on and found some soft, moist grass on the bank of the river. He helped himself to some. The grass tasted so refreshing that Tad wasn't paying attention to what he was doing. His back feet stepped on a patch of wet, slippery grass. He began sliding forward. He grabbed at the ground with his webbed feet, but couldn't get a hold of anything. He slid into the rapid current of the river headfirst.

The current swept him into a large boulder with a hard bang. He hit the boulder and was knocked unconscious. The river pushed him past the boulder into another smaller rock and then another before the water calmed and gently laid him on the bank.

Darkness was all around him when he awoke. In fact, the only thing that let him know he was awake was the pain in his head and neck. His eyes adjusted to the dim light and he could see he was lying on the bank of the river. At first, he couldn't remember anything and then he remembered munching on some very sweet grass.

Oh, yes, I remember losing my footing and sliding into the river. I must have banged into something, he thought to himself. *Ooooh, everything hurts so much.*

He laid his face back down in the moist dirt, moaning loudly.

He didn't realize it yet, but he had crossed the river into the magical side of Timberwood Forest. He was about to find out what Gail meant when she said magic sometimes doesn't turn out the way you plan.

That same evening, a gnome was walking home along the river. She walked with a limp because one leg was shorter than the other. Her foot caught the side of a stone which knocked her off balance and she fell.

"Oh, barnacles and Sasquatch!" Phlome exclaimed with frustration.

Falling was nothing new for Phlome because of her unsteady gait and the rocky floor of the forest. As she started to pull herself up, she noticed something lying on the bank of the river. Whatever it was appeared hurt.

"Hello there, lil' fella," she said, "what be ye?"

Tad moaned and tried to pull his head up to see who was talking to him.

Phlome went over to him and poked at him.

"I'm a turtle and I think I'm hurt," Tad replied.

"What's a turtle?" asked Phlome.

Tad was getting used to things not knowing what he was so he explained, "It's a creature with four legs, a head, a tail and a hard shell that crawls around on the ground real-ly slowly. Usually when I swim, I'm very nimble, but this water, it's so fast, it just took me where it wanted me to go."

"Ye be hurt?" asked Phlome.

"Yes. I'm not sure how badly, but everything hurts," answered Tad.

"Well, then, ye be comin' home with me," she said.

Tad had no choice, as at once he was in her hands and she was walking away. He relaxed into her grip because he was exhausted, and she seemed nice anyway. She tucked him into a loose pocket in her overcoat. She walked slowly and unsteadily up a long hill. When they got to the top of the hill, she pulled him out of her pocket. He had fallen asleep during the long walk.

"This is me home sweet home, lil' fella," she said.

He opened his sleepy eyes and saw a small cottage. She took him inside and set him on a rug. Then, she began making a fire in the fireplace. Next, she started mixing all kinds of different liquids into a glass. She was humming some strange words to herself, but Tad couldn't make them out. She brought the glass over to him and began pouring it down his throat.

She said, "Now, drink this up and get ye some sleep. Ye'll feel better in the mornin'."

As Tad drank the liquid, he began feeling warm all over. He wasn't sure if the warmth was from the liquid or the now roaring fire. But, he didn't feel any more pain. He yawned, stretched his arms and legs and fell asleep.

4 SOMETHING'S WRONG

In the morning, Tad woke up feeling better, but a little funny. Phlome was rocking in a rocking chair and looked over at him.

She said, "Good mornin' to ya, lil' fella. Hope ye are feelin' better. How about some breakfast to strengthen ye?"

She brought him a small bowl of food and

sat it down in front of him. He ate like he hadn't eaten in a week. Just then, there was a knock at the door. Phlome opened the door to a small man gnome. He had a concerned look on his face. He came in and shut the door behind him quietly.

Phlome said, "Hi, Thome. What's the matter with ye? Ye look like somethin's wrong?"

Thome put his forefinger to his lips and said, "*Sshhh*, there *is* somethin' wrong. The wizard left his castle. Word has it that somethin' has entered the magical forest. Ye know how the wizard feels about outsiders."

Phlome turned towards Tad and Thome's jaw dropped open when he saw him.

"Phlome, ye've got to get rid of whatever that be. You know how much trouble ye will be gettin' into for keepin' an outsider," Thome said.

Phlome said, "Ah, rats and bats, I thought he was kinda cute and I was goin' to be keepin' him as a pet. Poor lil' critter, he's all lost and scared. What should we do?"

"What should *we* do?" asked Thome, "No, I'm not involved in thisin here mess. The question is what are ye goin' to be doin'?"

Thome turned to leave. When he opened the door, a big black shadow covered the doorstep. He shut the door. "There be the wizard now!" Thome exclaimed.

They were all shaking, not knowing what was going to happen to them. They waited a few minutes and when nothing did happen, Phlome opened the door again. There was no shadow now, just a beautiful sunshiny day outside. Thome ran to the door when he realized the coast was clear nearly knocking Phlome down as he pushed past her to get out of the door.

"Ye be a big coward there, Thome," Phlome called after him, "thanks for all ye's help."

Phlome turned towards Tad, "Well, now I cain't be gettin' into trouble because of ye. Ye be goin' to have to leave."

"Where will I go?" Tad asked.

Phlome replied, "I'll take ye back down to the river. Ye can cross back over to the other side."

Tad said, "But, I've come this far. I have to see the wizard. I can't just leave without asking him for his help."

Phlome said, "Ye be askin' for a lot of trouble, lil' fella."

Tad said, "I just can't go back; You don't understand, nobody there likes me. I'm so slow, I can't even stand myself. I have to have the wizard's help to lose my shell and become as fast as a snake."

"Fish and fowl, Tad, ye be gettin' us both into a lot of trouble," Phlome said, "but I will take ye to the road that leads to the wizard's castle. After that, ye be on your own."

"Thank you, Phlome, you're a good friend," said Tad.

5 MAGIC

Phlome began packing up some things. She put on her overcoat and then picked up Tad and put him into her pocket. Then, they left the little cottage.

Phlome, in her usual way, hobbled along slowly, sometimes stumbling. Tad thought to himself how difficult it must be for her to walk around like that. Eventually, he stuck his head out of her pocket and said, "Phlome, I'm sorry you have difficulty getting around. I really appreciate you taking me to the road that leads to the castle."

Phlome replied, "Its ok, Tad. I've been this way a long time. I'm used to it by now. It's just difficult when I fall because I have a hard time trying to stand back up."

Tad had to ask the question, "But, do you mind that it takes you a long time to get where you're going?"

"Well, only when I be in a hurry which most times I ain't. I don't even usually think about how long it takes me to be gettin' somewhere. I just try to be keepin' my focus so I don't fall down," she replied.

Tad thought to himself about all the different ways of getting around from Mama Duck's waddling to Sherm the Worm's crawling on his belly, and Gail's home on her back. It seemed to him that everyone has something they struggle with but they make the best of it. They focus on the positive too, instead of the negative of their situation. But, Phlome, what positive thing did she have going for her? She was disabled. She had two legs that if they were perfectly matched up, she'd be able to run and play and do all the things the other gnomes could do. Yet, she didn't seem sad about her situation. She, too, seemed to make the most of it. He wanted to ask her how she came to have unmatched legs, but wasn't sure if he should. They went on in silence.

Phlome broke the silence by saying, "Whew, I be tired. Let's take a lil' break. What do ye say there lil' fella?"

Tad, who was anxious to get to the castle, wanted to keep going but he could tell that Phlome was tired because her breathing had become laborious, so he said, "Okay."

Phlome sat down on a nearby rock and pulled some snacks out of her bag. She ate some and fed some to Tad. Tad ate hungrily as if he'd been doing the walking.

Phlome said, "Tad, what is so important about going fast? You really seem unhappy with yourself."

Tad explained how the other animals would make fun of how slow he was and how his teacher, Mr. Peacock, would scold him for being late and make him stay after school which would make him even later getting home. He went on to explain how he met the snake who helped him see how wonderful it was to go fast without a shell. He wanted to be like that because then he could feel as free on land as he did in the water.

Phlome thought to herself and then asked, "So ye came to the magical forest to find the wizard so ye can be fast? Ye think that once ye are fast, ye life will be great?"

"Yes, that's it," said Tad. "I will be fast and free. It will be glorious!"

Phlome said, "Has anyone ever warned ye that magic doesn't always go as ye plan? It can be havin' some terrible consequences?"

Tad replied, "Yes, someone did, but mine won't. What can go wrong with wanting to be fast?"

Phlome said, "Ye be messin' with nature. Ye were made with a shell and made to be slow on land. Whenever ye mess with nature, it backfires. Ye see lil' fella, when I was a wee one, I worked in the castle. I saw the wizard do his magic. He's powerful, but nature is even more powerful."

"What do you mean?" Tad asked with interest.

Phlome's voice lowered, "I haven't spoken about this since I was wee, but I, too, had wished for magic to change me."

"Oh, really?" Tad asked.

"Yes," Phlome said, "and it backfired on me. I didn't like being a short lil' gnome. I wanted to be as tall as the wizard. One day I asked him to be changin' me. He warned me that I wasn't wishin' for a good thing. But, I had been a good servant. Plus, I kept askin' him. Eventually, he gave in. He cast a spell on me to make me tall, but this is all that happened. I gained one leg longer than ta other. Now, I'm worse off than I ever be. I've had to live with this hobble, walkin' slowly and fallin' down often. I've come to believen' that it wasn't a good thing to have been a wishin' to be different and that the two legs I had, even though they were short, were good legs. They had been servin' me well. I shouldn't have been wishin' them different."

"Oh," said Tad, "I'm sorry to hear about that. I had no idea that magic could make things worse. I thought it would give me everything I wanted. What am I going to do now?"

"Well, ye be welcome to go see the wizard, but I be thinkin' ye should go back home. Be thankful for ye shell and for goin' slow. There's much worse things to have than that," Phlome said.

Tad said soulfully, "Phlome, what you're saying is good and true. I need to think about this."

Phlome touched Tad's shell softly, "Ye shell is quite beautiful. In the sunlight showin' thru these here trees, it be real colorful."

Tad said, "Thank you, Phlome. No one has ever complimented my shell before."

They sat in silence for a while. Tad thought about everyone he had met and how they each had taught him something different about accepting the way that he's made, but he just didn't want to listen. Instead, he had listened to the snake, who made him believe magic would cure his unhappiness.

Finally, Tad said, "Well, Phlome, I guess I need to figure out a way to be happy just the way I am. And, I guess, I need to leave the magical forest because I don't think the wizard is too happy I'm here."

Phlome replied, "Well, lil' fella, I be thinkin' ye be right. I'll help ye get back to the river, but that's as far as I can go."

"Thanks," Tad said.

Phlome picked Tad up and put him in her pocket and started hobbling back the way they had come. A dark cloud covered the sky and Phlome pulled her jacket close around her neck.

"I be thinkin' it might be goin' to rain," said

Phlome.

A clap of thunder was heard overhead and small droplets started to fall. Lightening flashed and it began to pour down rain. Phlome was trying to hurry but the ground was so uneven she couldn't go too fast. Evening was approaching by the time she and Tad arrived back at her home. They were soaking wet.

"We'll have to be tryin' again tomorrow, lil' fella," Phlome said as she laid him down on the rug in front of the hearth again. She made a warm fire and they ate some soup before turning in to bed.

Tad thought about a lot of things as he was trying to go to sleep that night.

"Phlome, what did you use yesterday that seemed to help ease my pain?" Tad asked.

"Oh, that, I mixed up some herbs from the forest to be helpin' to ease the pain and fallin' asleep," Phlome replied.

"How did you learn about those herbs?"

asked Tad.

"When I worked with the wizard at the castle, he be usin' a lot of herbs in his magic potions. I learned whichin' ones did whichin' things. Now, don't you be worrin', there's nothin' magic in herbs. They be all natural. The great maker in the sky made them that way to help us," Phlome explained.

Tad asked, "Who's the great maker in the sky?"

Phlome replied, "The great maker in the sky be makin' everything. He made all things for us to be usin'. As long as we know what we be doin' and we're not usin' somethin' that doesn't really belong to us, like magic, to try and change what the great maker in the sky wants."

"How do you know what the great maker in the sky wants," asked Tad.

"Now, that be the question of the year there lil' fella. The point is ye don't always know what he be wantin', but ye know that the way he made ye is perfect. Even if it doesn't be seemin' so perfect," replied Phlome.

Tad thought about that for a while. If there was a great maker in the sky, maybe he was made perfect with a shell and webbed feet. Maybe wanting to be faster was not what he should be after. Maybe there was something else he should learn. Something that would help him accept himself the way he was and be happy.

With those thoughts in mind, Tad fell fast asleep.

6 THE WIZARD

In the morning, Phlome woke him up with a warm bowl of food. Tad ate breakfast with a new purpose in life. He wanted to figure out how to be happy with how he had been made.

Phlome could tell there was something different about Tad, so she asked, "What ye be thinkin' there, lil' fella?"

Tad replied, "Well, Phlome, I have learned a lot since I started trying to figure out how to be faster. I learned that other animals that are slow have figured out a way to be happy by focusing on what they do like about themselves. Like Mama Duck for instance, she doesn't focus on how she has to waddle when she walks, she is happy for her webbed feet when she swims. And Sherm the Worm doesn't worry about being fast, he enjoys feeling the cool dirt on his belly. Gail the Snail doesn't get upset when she can't get somewhere quickly, she enjoys having her home with her wherever she goes. I enjoy all those things too. I enjoy having webbed feet and being able to swim fast. I enjoy feeling cool dirt on my belly too. And Gail helped me to realize that having my home with me wherever I go is a great thing. My shell is a protection for me against disease and predators. And you, Phlome, you told me my shell was beautiful. I think I have a lot to be thankful for."

Phlome said, "Well, lil' fella, ye been doin' a lot of thinkin' and it seems ye have discovered that ye be made perfect after all."

Tad said, "Yes, I think I have been."

Phlome said, "Well, I be thinkin' it be time to get ye back to the river."

"Good idea, Phlome, let's go," said Tad.

So Tad and Phlome set out for the river. Phlome put on her overcoat and tucked Tad into her pocket. Tad and Phlome left the little cottage once again. Phlome hobbled down the side of the hill towards the river. The sun shone directly overhead by the time they reached the riverbank.

Phlome said, "Well, lil' fella, here's the river."

Tad said, "Yes, here it is."

Not wanting to leave Phlome just yet and a little scared to try to cross the river again, he said, "I'm a little hungry though. I think I'll munch on some of this yummy sweet grass before I try to cross that river again."

Phlome took out a morsel to eat too. She watched him munching and thought he was pretty special. She was glad she had helped him see that using magic to change himself wasn't the right answer. She was also glad for his friendship. He reminded her that there was a lot of good in this life.

Just then, a loud screech came from the sky. The wizard spotted him. The wizard swooped down and snatched him up off the ground.

Tad wasn't sure what had happened to him. He had heard a loud shriek and now he was high up in the sky and Phlome was getting smaller and smaller.

The wizard took him to his castle and dropped him on the cold, hard marble floor.

CRACK! went Tad's shell.

"*Ooowwwww!*" he cried.

Tad was lying on his back and couldn't get turned over. He was in a lot of pain, but didn't know that his shell had been broken.

The wizard landed on his feet and having the ability to read minds said in a loud, booming voice, "So, little turtle, you've come to the forest to find me. Well, you've found me. What did you think I could do for you?"

"I'm sorry, Mr. Wizard, sir," Tad said wincing in pain, "I didn't mean to come here to upset you. I was told by a snake who said you would grant my wish to be fast, but…."

Before he could finish his sentence, the Wizard interrupted and said, "So you want to be fast, do you?"

"Not anymore, Mr. Wizard, sir. I've come to realize that I was made perfect just the way I am," replied Tad.

"Where did you get that nonsense from? Phlome?" pried the Wizard.

"Phlome did help me to realize that, but there were other animals that had helped me too, I just didn't realize it before," Tad replied.

"Did you think you could just come to the magical forest and I wouldn't know? Did you think you could get me to do some magic on you without a price? What did you bring to pay me with?" boomed the Wizard.

"I didn't know what to think about the magical Timberwood Forest, nor about you. I didn't come with anything to offer," Tad said, suddenly realizing his mistake.

"Well, then, you shall be boiled to death in a pot of boiling water for violating my sacred decree that no one should enter my Magical Timberwood Forest without my permission and for someone who didn't even bring a payment, I shall make the water even hotter," The Wizard exclaimed loudly.

Tad was very scared. He couldn't get away because he was hurt and lying on his back. He waved his arms and legs to try and flip himself over, but there was nothing he could do. Then, two strong bodyguards of the wizard came over and grabbed him and took him outside to where large pot of boiling water was already started. He saw some other workers add wood to the flame underneath the pot.

"Please, Mr. Wizard, sir, please don't kill

me. I've learned my lesson that I'm ok just the way I am. I want to leave your forest and never come back," cried Tad.

"It's too late for that little turtle. You have violated my sacred decree and you must be put to death," commanded the Wizard.

"Isn't there another way?" Tad begged.

"No! Drop him in the water," the Wizard ordered.

"Wait!" a voice cried from behind.

The Wizard and Tad looked over where the voice had come from and saw Phlome standing there.

"Phlome, how did you get here?" asked Tad.

"Silence, turtle," the Wizard commanded and turning towards Phlome asked, "So, Phlome, you've come to save your little turtle friend?"

"That be whatin' I'm here for," replied Phlome, "Tad, is a sweet, innocent lil' fella who be given some bad advice. It's not his fault he's in your Magical Timberwood Forest without your permission. He be on his way home when ye grabbed him. It be my fault though that I be hidin' him."

The Wizard stated rhetorically, "Well, Phlome, you know that hiding a stranger in the Magical Timberwood Forest is a breach of my sacred decree, and is also punishable by death."

"Yes," said Phlome boldly, "do with me as ye wish, but let the lil' fella go."

"As you wish, Phlome," commanded the Wizard.

"No," pleaded Tad, "I won't let you die for me, Phlome. You were trying to help me and I'm the cause of all the trouble here. Take me instead."

"Well, now, don't we have an interesting dilemma? Maybe the two of you would like to go together!" boomed the Wizard.

Phlome said, "Ye know, I served ye faithfully for many a year. Then, one day I be makin' a mistake by askin' ye to perform magic on me which ye did against ye better judgment. Now, I live with one leg bein' shorter than ta other. I be usin' that experience to help Tad to be learnin' that magic isn't the way to solve anything. It's ye own personal belief that everythin' be happenin' for a reason. I be believin' now that my experience with magic happened so that I could be helpin' Tad. Why don't ye let Tad go so he can go back home and warn others. He be servin' ye better on the other side, warnin' others not to be comin' to your Magical Timberwood Forest.

Phlome's heart was beating hard, but she hoped her words would touch the Wizard.

The Wizard said, "You are right, Phlome. I do believe everything happens for a reason and maybe things happened just as they did to bring us here today. I am sorry for what you have to live with. That is punishment enough for you. I will grant your request to let Tad go."

"Thank you," said Phlome with a sigh of

relief.

The Wizard turned to Tad and said, "Today, I am granting the request of someone I harmed with my magic in order for you to warn others. I will let you go back to your home, but you must promise me that you will tell others of the dangers of magic."

"I will," Tad said, "Thank you, Mr. Wizard, sir. I will never forget your act of kindness this day."

Phlome went over to Tad and took him from the bodyguards and put him in her overcoat pocket. She hobbled a few steps and turned to look at the wizard. He had a sad look in his eyes. Together they made it back to Phlome's little cottage once again. Phlome cooked up a brew of special herbs to heal Tad's shell. He drank it up as they spoke about each other's bravery and how grateful they both were to be alive until they both fell fast asleep.

7 HEADED HOME

In the morning, Tad's shell was completely healed.

Tad said, "Wow, Phlome, you are great with those herbs. I'm as good as new!"

"I'm glad they be helpin', now let's be goin'," she said.

Tad and Phlome left once again for the river. When they got there, they paused to say good bye.

Phlome said, "Tad, it be a great pleasure

knowin' ye. I be wishin' ye the best for the rest of ye life. Don't be forgettin' about me and don't be forgettin' about the promise to the wizard. But most of all, cherish who ye are and how ye were made."

Tad said with a tear in his eye, "Phlome, you have been a great friend. Thank you so much for all you've taught me and for your act of bravery to die for me. I will never forget you and what you've done for me nor the words of the wizard. Good bye, my friend."

"Good bye, lil' fella," said Phlome.

With that, Tad dove into the river head first and swam with all his might. The river was wide and fast, but he swam with a renewed strength; a strength of knowing who he was and valuing himself the way he was made. When he reached the other side, he climbed out and looked back. He could barely see Phlome. He waved and she waved back. Then, she disappeared.

Tad made his way back through the forest

turning at the third oak and past the lilac patches thinking about all that had happened to him. He reached the pond the following day. He stopped on the bank and thought about the strong river he had swam through just the day before. He was new today, new inside. He liked himself. He dove into the pond and swam and sang, "Swishing here, swishing there, I can swim anywhere."

FROM THE AUTHOR

I appreciate you taking the time to read *A Turtle's Magical Adventure*. If you enjoyed it, please consider telling your friends or posting a short review on Amazon.com. Word of mouth is an author's best friend and much appreciated.

Thank you.

Wanda Luthman

If you'd like to connect with me and receive a free exclusive Ebook, visit my website at www.wandaluthman.wordpress.com and sign up for my newsletter.